The Woodland Gospels

according to Captain Beaky
and his Band

by Jeremy Lloyd

Illustrated by Graham Percy
Foreword by
the Archbishop of Canterbury

faber and faber
LONDON·BOSTON

First published in 1984 by Faber and Faber Limited
3 Queen Square London WC1N 3AU
Printed in Great Britain by Jolly & Barber Ltd, Rugby, Warwickshire

Inquiries about all rights in the material in *The Woodland Gospels*,
other than book publishing rights, should be addressed to
London Management, 235 Regent Street, London W1A 2JT

Captain Beaky TM is the registered trademark of Captain Beaky Limited

British Library Cataloguing in Publication Data

Lloyd, Jeremy | The Woodland gospels according to Captain Beaky and his band.
I. Title | 823'.914[J]   PZ7 | ISBN 0-571-13270-7

Library of Congress Cataloging in Publication Data | Lloyd, Jeremy.
The Woodland Gospels according to Captain Beaky and his band.
Summary: Captain Beaky and his Band set out to spread
the teachings of Jesus to the creatures of the forest.
[1. Christian life — Fiction]   I. Percy, Graham, ill.
II. Title. | PZ7.L7776Wo   1984 | [Fic] | 83-20790 | ISBN 0-571-13270-7

FOREWORD
by the Archbishop of Canterbury

You might think, at first, that Captain Beaky, Artful Owl, Reckless Rat and Timid Toad would make strange disciples of Our Lord: and yet, after all, He was born in a stable and among His first admirers must have been the animals with whom he shared it. So perhaps Captain Beaky and his Band do have something special to share with all of us, both children and adults. I hope you will enjoy the story of Jesus told in this new and exciting way.

+ ROBERT CANTUAR

J ust a few minutes before four o'clock on a hot afternoon in the Woods, Captain Beaky and his Band — that is, Artful Owl, Timid Toad and Reckless Rat — were sitting under a large candy-striped umbrella outside Owl's tree house. Above them, hanging from a low branch, was Batty Bat. They were there because Owl was about to serve tea on the lawn, and the rattle of cups as he came down the winding wooden stairs woke up Timid Toad. Toad had been dreaming that Hissing Sid, the most evil snake in the Woods, was tiny and that he, Toad, was a giant with a big fly swat, and that he had been busy swatting Sid as he fled to safety down his hole.

'Tea's ready at last,' said Rat.

'I'm very thirsty,' said Toad.

'So am I,' said Captain Beaky, 'so I hope there's plenty of tea, and plenty of cakes.'

'And two kinds of jam,' squeaked Batty Bat, 'just in case I don't like one.'

'You are very fortunate,' said Owl, as he stepped from the doorway of the big old tree holding a large tray, 'to be getting any tea at all.'

'What do you mean?' said Reckless Rat, as he tied knots in the four corners of a big red hanky. 'We always have tea on a Saturday afternoon.' And, pulling the hanky firmly down on to his head, he stood up and helped Owl to lay the cups and saucers and the teapot and the plates of cakes and bread and butter and two kinds of jam on the crisp white tablecloth that was spread on the lawn.

'You are fortunate,' said Owl, 'because I am busy at the moment preparing my sermon to read in church.'

'That's not till next week,' said Captain Beaky, picking up a napkin and tying it around his neck.

'That may be so,' said Owl, 'but being perhaps the cleverest person in the Woods, I am expected to give a particularly good sermon; in fact, I'm surprised Mr Vole the Vicar hasn't asked me before this,' and, lifting up the large brown teapot, he began to fill the cups.

Reckless Rat leant forward, picking the only cake with a cherry on top.

'Perhaps it's because we hardly ever go to church,' he said.

'We were all in church last Tuesday,' said Captain Beaky.

'Agreed,' said Rat, 'but only because we were chasing Hissing Sid, who ran in the front and out the back.'

Timid Toad, Artful Owl and Batty Bat both took two cakes each, and Captain Beaky grabbed the last cake before Reckless Rat could get it.

'Tell us, Owl,' he said, 'what sort of subject have you in mind?'

'Greed,' said Owl.

'Oh,' said Captain Beaky, putting the cake back on the plate.

'That's a good subject,' said Rat, picking it up and taking a large bite.

'The problem is,' said Owl, spreading one of the two kinds of jam on a piece of bread, 'that there is so much to choose from in the Bible.'

'Apart from which,' said Captain Beaky, 'we all know it.'

'Do we?' said Owl.

'Of course,' said Captain Beaky. 'How God made the world in only seven days.'

'Six days,' said Rat. 'He was worn out, so he went to bed on the seventh.'

'Well, six days,' said Captain Beaky.

'He made Adam and Eve,' said Timid Toad, 'and gave them a lovely garden to live in.'

'Go on,' said Owl, 'tell us about it.'

'Well,' said Toad, 'it was probably like these Woods only better, and they had everything they could want.'

'Two kinds of jam?' squeaked Bat.

'Everything,' said Toad. 'But God asked them not to eat the apples off his best tree.'

'It wasn't his best tree,' said Owl. 'It was a special tree.'

'It was the Tree of Knowledge,' said Captain Beaky knowingly.

'We all know that,' said Rat, 'and we all know that a snake, probably Hissing Sid's great-great-great-great-great-grandfather, was the one who said, "Psst — hey, no one's looking, Eve, have a nibble," and she did. And then she let Adam have a bite, and God was not pleased, and they were turned out of the garden.'

'I have never known why eating one apple was such a serious thing,' said Toad.

'It's an example,' said Owl. 'If a very wise person tells you not to do something, you must not do it. That apple, as Captain Beaky said, was from the Tree of Knowledge — one bite and they knew everything, and God knew that to know too much before you're ready to know it can be a bad thing. For example, if you show a baby how to strike a match before it understands the danger of fire, what could happen?'

'He could set his hat on fire,' said Rat. 'Which, if he was wearing it at the time, could be dangerous.'

'Anyway,' said Captain Beaky, 'that was all a very long time ago. Now we know most things and how to behave; it's called being civilized.'

'I agree,' said Rat. 'That's why not many people go to church today — because they think they know everything.'

'Exactly,' said Owl. 'Apart from which, Mr Vole the Vicar does tend to fall asleep while he's giving the sermon.'

'Perhaps,' said Timid Toad, 'he's tired of telling the same story.'

'That's the point I'm trying to make,' said Owl. 'I don't think people listen any more. There are a lot of lessons to be learnt from the Bible that apply today, but people aren't interested.'

'I fly to the top of a tree and say my prayers every night,' said Batty Bat, 'and I know God listens.'

'How?' said Captain Beaky.

'Because,' said Bat, 'I always ask for two kinds of jam at Owl's house and I always get them.'

Artful Owl shook his head. 'I despair of you all,' he said, 'and if we are the cleverest animals in these Woods, as we have often mentioned amongst ourselves, what are the rest of the inhabitants like?'

'They are like us,' said Rat, 'and, like us, they don't need to read the Bible quite so often, 'cos nowadays the world's a much better and kinder place than it used to be.' And picking up a plate he swatted a wasp with it.

'That was very unkind,' said Owl.

'I agree,' said Toad.

'We should be kind to creatures great and small,' said Captain Beaky, 'like it says in the Bible.'

'Surely,' said Owl, 'a lowly wasp has as much right to a bit of jam as we have.'

'Sorry about that,' said Rat. 'I didn't think. Tell you what — we'll give him a nice burial.' And, lifting the plate, he bent down and peered at the wasp. Pandemonium broke out as the bad-tempered wasp buzzed angrily around their heads.

'Get it!' shouted Captain Beaky. 'It's flying round me.'

'It's after me!' cried Toad, hopping up and down.

'Mind my best teapot,' said Owl.

Batty Bat hurried away to the safety of Owl's staircase. Finally the wasp landed on Captain Beaky's hat.

'Don't move,' said Reckless Rat and, holding up his plate and aiming carefully, he brought it down with a loud thud. 'I definitely got it that time,' said Rat.

It was nearly five minutes before Captain Beaky's headache was better and most of the stars had disappeared.

'Are you better now?' said Owl.

'Not much,' said Captain Beaky.

'So much for the Bible,' said Rat. 'If it hadn't said be kind to all things great and small, that would never have happened.'

'If,' said Toad, 'you hadn't been unkind to that wasp in the first place, it wouldn't have been cross.'

'You might as well say,' said Rat, 'that if Batty Bat hadn't prayed for two kinds of jam, it wouldn't have come sniffing round here to begin with.'

Owl poured himself another cup of tea. 'I'm very worried about my sermon,' said Owl. 'Not that it won't be good, but that people who come to hear it will come not because they are interested but because they always come.'

'The ones that always come,' said Rat, 'know it all anyway.'

'Exactly,' said Owl. 'Now, what we should do is to take the good word into the Woods, to the people who don't come to church.'

'Good idea,' said Captain Beaky. 'In fact, I was just about to suggest it myself.'

'You mean, like Jesus did?' said Timid Toad.

'What better example could we have?' said Owl. 'We'll tell them stories from the Gospels.'

'And if they don't listen,' said Rat, 'I'll punch them on the nose.'

'I don't think you were cut out for the Church,' said Owl.

Batty Bat, who had flapped back again, hung from the umbrella and nodded in agreement. 'When do we start?' he squeaked.

'Well, we've been busy all week doing good in the Woods,' said Owl, 'so I think we should start on Monday. In the meantime I suggest you all look at the Gospels just to remind yourselves what they're about.'

'When should we do that?' said Toad.

'How about tomorrow?' said Captain Beaky.

'It's Sunday tomorrow,' said Rat. 'We're all supposed to rest, according to the Bible, so I suggest we do a bit of revision on Monday and start on Tuesday.'

'That settles it,' said Owl. 'That is a typical example of sloth.'

Rat looked puzzled. 'Sloth — what's that?'

'Laziness,' said Owl.

'Why didn't you say so?' said Rat.

'If God had been like you,' said Owl, 'and had kept putting off making the world till tomorrow, there wouldn't be one.'

'Yes, there would,' squeaked Bat, 'except today would be Sunday.'

'In that case,' said Owl, 'we'll start today.'

'Today!' said Toad. 'But it's after tea-time!'

'Now,' said Owl. 'Right now. I'll get my Woodland Bible.'

'Yes,' said Captain Beaky. 'It's time we did something really good.'

And so Captain Beaky and his Band, that is, Artful Owl, Reckless Rat, Timid Toad and Batty Bat, set out on a Saturday afternoon after tea to bring the Gospels to the Woodland World. As it turned out, they started later than they had intended because, as Rat pointed out, they might be out late, and he wanted to lock up his house in case someone like Hissing Sid broke in.

Timid Toad had to go to his home down by the river to get a scarf in case it was a cold night. Batty Bat said he'd just pop his piece of bread and jam into his larder in case the wasps found it. And Captain Beaky explained that he had to go home to get his picnic hamper in case they got hungry — and also to get his firefly lantern in case it was a dark night.

'We'll all meet,' said Captain Beaky, 'at the Woodland Crossroads in half an hour.'

'That should just give me enough time to clear away the tea things and do the washing-up,' said Owl. 'Unless you all want to stay and help me now.'

'I think,' said Captain Beaky, 'the sooner we bring the Gospels to the Woodland folk the better. All those in favour raise their hands.'

All except Artful Owl raised their hands.

Exactly half an hour later Artful Owl stood at the Woodland Crossroads. He was holding his Bible under one arm and was dressed in his best nightshirt. A whistle made him turn round. Captain Beaky appeared, wearing his very best hat and struggling with a large picnic basket. He was also carrying a lantern, a telescope and a map rolled up under his arm. 'Map of the Woods,' he cried, waving it in the air. 'Quite a few places we haven't been to for a long time.'

'That's true,' said Artful Owl and, producing a small mirror and a comb from his nightshirt, he combed his big white eyebrows until they stood straight up in the air. Captain Beaky gazed at Artful Owl's nightshirt in some surprise.

'Are you having an early night?' said Captain Beaky.

'No,' said Owl, 'but I feel that as we are passing on, as it were, the words of the Gospels, we should look important. This nightshirt was very expensive.'

'In that case,' said Captain Beaky, 'as leader of this Band I should wear it.'

'It happens to be mine and it won't go with your hat,' said Owl. 'Ah, here comes Timid Toad.'

'Oh dear,' said Captain Beaky, 'I think he's hurt his leg.'

They both watched with concern as Timid Toad walked towards them leaning on a freshly cut forked stick. Like Owl, he also wore a nightshirt, but it only came to his knees. On his feet were a large pair of sandals made of string and leather that flapped about as he walked, and round his neck was a small woollen scarf.

'Poor Toad, what's the matter?' asked Captain Beaky.

'Nothing,' said Toad.

'What do you need the stick for?' said Owl.

'It's my staff,' said Toad. 'In the Bible all the prophets had one of these. I expect it was to lean on when they talked to people, and I thought it would make me look more important — that's why I wore my best nightshirt and these sandals.'

'You look ridiculous,' said Owl.

'Do I?' asked Toad anxiously. 'I thought I looked quite well dressed.'

'You do,' said Captain Beaky. 'Owl's just cross because he didn't think of a stick.'

'Hello, there,' said a familiar voice. Reckless Rat was wearing his best dressing-gown. The red hanky which he'd worn knotted on his head was now ironed and flapped smartly from his top pocket, and he had brushed his hair with great care. In his hands he carried two forked sticks.

'I brought these for you and me,' Rat said, handing one to Captain Beaky, 'so the people we talk to will know we're important, just like they did in the Bible, when the prophets were walking about telling everyone what was and what wasn't.'

'Thank you,' said Captain Beaky and, choosing the longer one, he leaned on it and studied his map.

Artful Owl took out his comb and combed his eyebrows down over his eyes.

'Where's that stupid Bat?' he asked crossly.

'I'm here,' squeaked Batty Bat and, flapping down, he hung from the end of Captain Beaky's stick. 'I'm ready,' he squeaked.

'Right,' said Captain Beaky, 'let's go.'

'Just a moment,' said Artful Owl and, reaching up, he removed from a low branch the largest, most important-looking straw hat that any of them had ever seen and placed it on his head. 'I'm ready now,' said Owl, 'but I must point out that it looks rather odd for everyone to be carrying a stick except me.'

'In that case,' said Captain Beaky, 'you can carry the basket.'

Before Artful Owl could protest Captain Beaky handed him the large picnic basket.

Raising his stick, he cried, 'Follow me!'

And so Captain Beaky and his Band marched through the Woods singing their favourite song and looking for anyone who would listen to the story they had to tell. But the inhabitants of the Woods were used to Captain Beaky and his Band singing songs and marching about, and so no one came to see if anything special was going on. After an hour they were rather hot and tired.

'I must sit down,' said Toad.

'So must I,' said Owl. Collapsing under a tree, he examined his foot and removed a twig from between his toes. He threw it over his shoulder.

'We should have started later,' he said, 'when it's cooler.'

'It's later now,' said Rat, 'and it's still hot.' And, undoing his dressing-gown, he removed his hanky and mopped his brow with it.

'What we should do,' said Captain Beaky, 'is make people come to us.'

'Isn't that why they built churches,' said Timid Toad, 'so people would know where to go?'

'Be quiet,' said Owl, 'I'm thinking.'

'So am I,' said Captain Beaky.

'We need,' said Artful Owl, 'a bell or something to attract attention.'

'Like they have in a church?' said Toad.

'Shut up, Toad,' said Captain Beaky, 'and leave the brain work to us.'

'Got it,' said Owl. 'I've just remembered. There's an old biscuit tin down by the river bank, near the old boat. All we have to do is hit it with our sticks and people will come to see what's going on.'

'And then,' said Captain Beaky, 'we can tell them all about Jesus.'

'Wouldn't it be easier to go to the church and ring the bell,' asked Toad, 'and tell them when they came there?'

'Give me your stick,' said Owl. 'It's too big for you.' And, despite Timid Toad's protests, Artful Owl took his stick and led the way to the river.

'There's the old boat,' said Captain Beaky, pointing to the remains of an upturned wooden boat on the bank.

'Where's the biscuit tin?' asked Bat.

'It's stuck out there on a mudbank,' said Rat. 'Must have fallen in the river.'

'So much for that idea,' said Rat.

'I know this part of the river,' said Toad. 'There's a log stuck between this bank and that mudbank.'

Reckless Rat shaded his eyes. 'I can't see it,' he said.

'It's just under the water,' said Toad. 'I know exactly where it is — I could easily walk out there and get that tin.'

'That's the first time you've been useful today,' said Owl.

As they scrambled down to the river's edge, Old Badger, who knew everything and everybody, everything that happened in the Woods and everybody in them, came towards them. He peered short-sightedly, not recognizing them at first.

'Ah, it's you lot,' said Old Badger. 'Is there a fancy-dress party tonight I don't know about?'

'No,' said Captain Beaky. 'We are teaching the Gospels and looking for people who need to be reminded of the story of Jesus.'

'Story of what?' said Old Badger, cupping his hand to his ear.

'Jesus,' said Artful Owl. 'How he was born and what happened to him.'

'And,' said Captain Beaky, 'how he performed miracles like walking on the water and healing the sick.'

'And how they killed him,' said Rat, 'after all he'd done for them.'

'Who?' said Old Badger.

'Jesus,' said Captain Beaky. 'It's all here in the Bible.' And, taking Owl's Bible, he waved it under Old Badger's nose.

'Ah, Jesus,' said Old Badger, nodding. 'He promised to come back.'

'That's right,' said Artful Owl. 'I'm glad some of the seeds sown haven't fallen on barren ground.'

'We are here,' said Captain Beaky, 'to tell everybody about it.'

'Has he come back then?' said Old Badger excitedly. 'Because if he has, I must run home and tell the wife.'

Captain Beaky took hold of Badger's ear and spoke slowly into it.

'Old Badger,' he said, 'we are gathered here to remind all the people of the story told in the Gospels.'

'Ah,' said Old Badger. 'I heard that very clear. What people?'

'WE ARE ABOUT TO ATTRACT THEIR ATTENTION,' said Artful Owl in a loud voice. 'Toad, get the biscuit tin.'

Timid Toad stepped down to the river bank, peering carefully to make sure he was at the right spot, and stepped cautiously on to the hidden log. Holding his arms out to keep his balance, he walked towards the tin.

19

Halfway there he paused, wobbled a bit, but kept his balance and continued. Old Badger's eyes stood out on stalks. 'He's come back,' shouted Badger, 'and he's walking on the water! Well I never!' And before they could stop him, he ran into the woods shouting, 'Jesus is back just like he promised, and he's a lot smaller than I thought he was.' And with a rustling of leaves and a cracking of twigs, he disappeared into the undergrowth.

'One must remember,' said Owl, 'that we are dealing with very simple people.'

'I've got it!' shouted Timid Toad and, pulling the old biscuit tin behind him, he walked back to the bank. 'What was all that commotion about?'

'Nothing,' said Owl. 'A misunderstanding.' He dug Toad's stick into the soft river bank, and then he placed the biscuit tin upside-down on the end.

'Right,' said Captain Beaky. 'Now Rat and I will bang on the tin with our sticks to attract people's attention.'

Startled birds flew from the trees, fish swam to the bottom of the river, and there was a crackling in the undergrowth as small animals in the vicinity ran for their lives from the loud din.

Batty Bat, who was hovering high above them to report on the appearance of the first animals, squeaked out the bad news.

'Oh dear,' said Owl, 'it seems this noise has frightened everyone off.'

Batty Bat flapped down. 'Whose idea was it?' asked Bat. 'I forget.'

'Owl's,' said Captain Beaky, 'and not a very good one.'

'No one has to be right all the time,' said Owl, 'and if I have any failing, it is to assume that other people are as intelligent as I am.'

Just then a sudden gust of wind indicated a change of weather. A black cloud appeared and a few heavy drops of rain fell.

'Oh,' said Timid Toad, 'perhaps we should go home if it's going to rain.'

'It's not *going* to,' said Rat. 'It *is*!'

'In that case,' said Captain Beaky, 'I suggest we take shelter under this old upturned boat here, and use some of these dry bits of wood to light a nice fire.' Crawling under the boat, he beckoned to the others. With the aid of a box of matches and a lot of puffing from Timid Toad and flapping from Batty Bat, they got a small fire going and sat round it.

'Things could be worse,' said Owl, wiggling his toes as he warmed his feet.

'Could they?' asked Bat, wrapping his wings tightly round himself.

'Well,' said Timid Toad, taking off his wet sandals and putting them by the fire to dry, 'so much for bringing the Gospels to the Woods.'

'I feel,' said Owl, 'that perhaps we should take this opportunity to discuss the subject amongst ourselves, just to make sure that we all know what we are talking about.'

'Ask me a question,' said Rat. 'Anything, because I have read the Bible from beginning to end.'

Owl opened the Bible and, taking a small pair of spectacles out of his pocket, he popped them on the end of his nose. 'Who was John the Baptist's father?' said Owl.

'Pass,' said Rat.

'What was the name of the Roman Emperor at the time of the birth of Jesus?' asked Owl.

'Pass,' said Rat.

'You don't know very much, do you?' said Captain Beaky.

'I know all the important bits,' said Rat. 'I mean, it makes no difference to the story who was Emperor. All we have to know are the important bits, like what Jesus said and did.'

'His father was a carpenter called Joseph,' said Toad, 'and his mother was called Mary.'

'We all know that,' said Rat, 'but if his father had been a plumber, it wouldn't have made any difference.'

'It would have made a difference,' said Toad. 'They'd have had to spend a lot more on furniture.'

'These details are of no importance,' said Owl.

'Exactly,' said Rat. 'That is the point I was trying to make. Now, as I see it, what matters is that God arranged for Jesus to come down to earth in a special way, and that special way was to make him the baby son of a lady who wasn't married yet.'

'Cuckoos are doing it all the time,' squeaked Bat.

'Doing what?' said Rat.

'Laying eggs in other people's nests, and letting them look after their kids.'

'I think,' said Captain Beaky, 'that we should make it clear to Batty Bat, just in case he's not sure, that God is not a cuckoo and that the Virgin Mary was not about to lay an egg.'

'Even Bat isn't that stupid,' said Owl.

'I am,' said Bat.

'May I continue?' said Owl. 'The important thing here is that God sent an angel to tell Mary what he'd done, and then he sent another one to tell Joseph that the girl he was going to marry was going to have a baby who would be famous for ever and ever because he would be the Son of God.'

'I bet Joseph was dying to tell the neighbours,' said Timid Toad. 'I would.'

'Visiting angels are a very private matter,' said Owl, 'and he did not tell the neighbours. And Mary and Joseph got married straight away — in fact, the angels had even told both of them what the baby's name was to be.'

'Baby Jesus,' said Toad.

'Brilliant,' said Rat. 'Of course it was Baby Jesus — that's who the story's about. And we know that his father and mother travelled on a donkey to a place called Bethlehem, and when they got there all the places to stay were full, so they had to sleep in a stable where the animals slept. And that's where Jesus was born, and that's where the Three Wise Men came to see him, to make sure he was who they thought he was.'

'All babies look the same,' said Bat, 'so how could they tell?'

'Because there was a star over Bethlehem, and that star was right over the stable,' said Owl, glancing at the open book on his knee. 'Now, the local king, who was called Herod, heard about Jesus being born because wise men had arrived from far and wide asking where their new king was. As he was a king himself, he didn't want any other kings about.'

'Not even a baby king?' said Toad.

'I'm afraid not,' said Owl. 'Now, Herod didn't know exactly where Jesus was, so he had all the little children in Bethlehem put to death. But the soldiers never thought of looking for a king in a stable, so Mary and Joseph managed to escape with Jesus.'

Timid Toad pulled Rat's hanky out of his pocket and wiped his eyes.

'Poor little children,' said Toad. 'How could people be so bad to them?'

'Well,' said Rat, 'bad people are frightened of good people 'cos they know that good people will always win in the end.'

'That's true,' said Owl, 'but good people who are really good suffer more than the bad people, because they know what is good and bad, and bad people only know what is bad.'

There was silence for a moment.

'That's very profound,' said Rat, 'and if I had a pencil I'd write that down — if I could write.'

'What happened to Jesus?' said Bat. 'Did he become a plumber like his father?'

'A carpenter,' said Owl. 'Yes, he did, but he spent a lot of time going to the temple, where clever men taught people about God, and he became clever like them while he was still a boy.'

'Some people,' observed Rat, 'have a natural gift for learning.'

'I wish I had,' said Toad. 'I forget everything, unless of course I'm interested — I mean, really interested — and then I remember it.'

'Are you interested in the story?' asked Owl.

'I am,' said Toad.

'Then shut up,' said Rat.

'Well,' said Owl, 'according to the Bible, quite a few years passed and Jesus grew into a man. By then, of course, he was very wise. Now, in the desert, a long way from where Jesus lived, was a prophet called John the Baptist, who'd been told by an angel that God's son would soon pay him a visit.'

'They were very busy people, these angels,' said Bat. 'If they hadn't told everyone what was going on, nobody would have known anything!'

'If nobody had bothered to write the Bible,' said Rat, 'nobody would have known anything about all this anyhow, so that was a silly remark.'

'May I continue?' said Owl.

'Be my guest,' said Rat.

'Well,' continued Owl, 'John the Baptist told everyone he met that God's son was on his way and warned them to behave themselves and, if they were bad, to change their ways. John the Baptist knew so much, and he was so kind, that some people thought *he* was God's son, and they asked him if he was.'

'Was he?' said Bat.

'Of course he wasn't,' said Owl. 'You're not listening.'

'God could have had two sons,' said Bat. 'Mrs McFerret had sixteen.'

Captain Beaky scratched his head. 'What's that got to do with John the Baptist?' he said

'Nothing,' said Bat. 'I was just mentioning it because it was such a surprise to her.'

'Now,' said Owl, 'Jesus heard about John the Baptist, and he travelled a long way to see him. When Jesus found him, John the Baptist was standing in the river baptizing people.'

'What's baptizing people?' said Bat.

'It's like christening,' said Owl. 'He put water on their heads and forgave them for their sins.'

Batty Bat used a wing to scoop up some rainwater and poured it over his head. 'I feel better for that,' he said. 'Wetter but better.'

'I'm glad to hear it, though that's not quite the same thing as baptizing,' said Owl. 'Now, when Jesus got to the river, he asked John the Baptist to baptize him. And as soon as John saw Jesus, he knew he was the son of God.'

'Did an angel tell him?' said Toad.

'No,' said Owl, 'he just knew. He just knew by looking at him, because Jesus was the most special person in the world, and John said to Jesus that he knew he wasn't as good as Jesus, and he asked Jesus to baptize him. But Jesus insisted, and he knelt down in the water of the river, and John baptized him. And the moment he'd done it, Jesus heard God's voice for the first time, and the voice said' — and Owl here lowered his voice so that it echoed around the upturned boat — ' "You are my own dear son and I am pleased with you." '

'That sent a tingle down my back,' said Toad.

'What did?' said Captain Beaky.

'When Owl did that deep voice, I can imagine that's just what God sounds like,' said Toad.

'How do you know?' said Rat. 'His voice might sound like mine or Bat's.'

'You've got a common voice,' said Toad.

'What makes you think,' asked Rat, 'that God speaks all la-di-da? He could speak like me if he wanted to. I mean, if he wanted to have a chat with me, and if I spoke Hindustani, he'd speak to me in Hindustani. And it wouldn't be posh Hindustani!'

'I think we're agreed,' said Captain Beaky, 'that for the purpose of this story Owl does God's voice very well. It's easy to understand.'

'Thank you,' said Owl, turning the page and peering at it. 'Could you light a candle or two? It's getting dark in here.' And after a search in the picnic basket, Captain Beaky found a long candle and lit it.

'That's better,' said Owl, and as their shadows flickered on to the sides of the boat, he continued with the story of Jesus.

'Now,' said Owl. 'Jesus was so moved by hearing his father's voice that he walked off into the desert, and he spent forty days and forty nights there until he grew weak with hunger.'

'I wonder why,' said Rat.

'I know why,' said Bat. 'It was because he hadn't eaten anything.'

'I mean,' said Rat, 'why did he want to spend all that time alone?'

'Because,' said Owl, 'he knew when he heard God's voice that he was indeed the most special person in the world, and that was a great responsibility, and he needed time to think about it. And at his weakest moment,' said Owl, 'from nowhere there appeared the Devil himself, whose name was Satan.'

'Oh,' said Toad, holding Rat's hand, 'what do you think he looked like?'

Owl gazed at the candle. 'He had the most evil face in the world,' said Owl. 'He had the face of a goat, with great horns, and his feet were cloven hooves. And his eyes glowed like burning coals.'

'Does it say so in there, in that Bible?' said Rat.

'No,' said Owl.

'In that case,' said Rat, 'who's to say that he didn't look like you or me?'

'Come to think of it,' said Toad, letting go of Rat's hand, 'he could have looked like you.'

'Whatever he looked like,' said Captain Beaky, 'I'm sure it wasn't very nice.'

'And the Devil,' said Owl, obviously enjoying his role as the storyteller, 'spoke to Jesus and said —' Owl took a very deep breath, turned over a page, then turned it back again.

'I can't stand the suspense,' whispered Toad. 'What *did* the Devil say?'

'Wait a moment,' muttered Owl. 'I've lost my place. Ah, here we are — and the Devil said. . .' Owl lowered his voice to almost a hiss, '". . . If you are the son of God, satisfy your hunger. Turn these desert rocks into bread and eat. If you are God's son, you can have anything you ask for."'

'Including two kinds of jam?' said Bat.

'If Owl does that voice again,' said Toad, 'I'm going home.' Picking up his sandals, he started to put them on.

'Be quiet,' said Captain Beaky. 'What did Jesus do?'

'Punched him on the nose,' said Rat.

29

'No,' said Owl, 'he just kept on walking, and he said to the Devil, "Man can't live by bread alone." And the Devil put an arm around Jesus, and swept him up to the top of the highest mountain, and showed him the whole world, and said, "If you will worship me, all this and everything in it is yours." Then Jesus told Satan to get out of his sight because there was only one God and that was his father. And the Devil turned into a whirling cloud of dry leaves, and a strong wind blew him away.'

'How did Jesus get down?' said Bat.

'He climbed down,' said Rat. 'How else could he get down?'

'Well,' said Bat, 'with all those angels about, one could have rescued him.'

'He could have taken the string out of his sandals,' said Toad, 'and tied them to his robe and sort of parachuted down.'

'He did *not* parachute down,' said Owl.

'Well, he must have got down somehow,' said Captain Beaky.

'A big eagle rescued him,' said Owl, 'and carried him down.'

'Does it say that in the Bible?' said Rat.

'No,' said Owl, 'but it doesn't matter how he got down. What matters is that he resisted all the Devil's temptations, which would have given him an easy life, and that is why he was so special. Anyway, Jesus went home to Nazareth, where he lived, and gave up being a carpenter.'

'Why, wasn't he any good?' said Bat.

'Of course he was good,' said Owl, 'but he had more important things to do than make chairs and tables, so he walked into the local temple and started to preach — but they threw him out.'

'They wouldn't have thrown me out,' said Rat. 'I'd have banged their heads together and made them listen.'

Artful Owl gave a sigh. 'After banging their heads together, it would have been very hard to convince people that you were God's son, who'd arrived to bring peace to this earth.'

'Put like that,' said Rat, 'I suppose you're right.'

'The reason why they wouldn't let him preach,' said Owl, 'was that most people didn't think a humble carpenter could teach them anything. So Jesus went into the countryside to preach, and some people did listen, and among them were four fishermen he met by Lake Galilee. Can anyone remember their names because they are important to the story?'

'Let me see,' said Rat.

'On the tip of my tongue,' said Beaky.

Bat tried hard to think of an important name. 'Got it,' said Bat. 'Charles — was one called Charles?'

'No one in the Bible was called Charles,' said Owl. 'The fishermen were Simon and his brother Andrew, and two other brothers, James and John. They became his followers, but only after he had performed a miracle to convince them who he was.'

'He walked on the water,' said Rat.

'No, that was later,' said Owl.

'He saved his best ones till last,' said Captain Beaky. 'I'd have done that.'

'What Jesus did,' said Owl, 'was to gather so many fish together near the shore that the fishermen nearly broke their nets catching them.'

'It could just have been a good day for fishing,' said Bat.

'It was a bad day,' said Owl. 'But there were lots more miracles to come. And every time Jesus did a miracle, the news spread.'

'What would you call a miracle?' asked Bat.

'If you could understand anything we were talking about,' said Rat, 'that would be a miracle.'

'He healed a leper,' said Owl.

'What's a leper?' asked Bat.

'Someone with leprosy,' said Owl. 'It's a very bad illness.'

'Is it worse than measles?' asked Toad.

'It's a lot worse,' said Owl. 'But Jesus just placed his hand on him and he got better. And the leper told everyone, and all the sick people came to be healed. And as the news spread, more and more followers joined Jesus until there were twelve of them.'

'It's stopped raining,' said Bat, peering out from under the boat.

'I vote we stay here,' said Captain Beaky. 'It's rather fun, like camping out, and I think old Owl makes the Bible very interesting.'

'So do I,' said Toad. 'I wish I'd met Jesus. I don't think I've ever met a really special person — apart from all of you, of course.'

'Shush,' said Rat. 'Unless I'm mistaken, we're not alone.'

'W-w-what is it?' stammered Toad, peering into the gloom.

'I can see a pair of eyes,' said Rat, 'and they're staring at us.'

31

'What if it's the Devil,' whispered Toad, 'and he catches us reading the Bible?'

'Don't be silly,' said Captain Beaky. 'Anyway, we're not reading it, Owl is.' Owl peered over his spectacles into the gloom. 'It's that snake, Hissing Sid,' he said, 'and he's spying on us.'

'I'm not spying,' hissed Sid. 'I was listening. It's the best story I've ever heard. Can I join you?'

'Join us?' said Rat. 'Certainly not!'

'Hold on,' said Owl. 'He may be bad, but we should try and help him. Let him in.'

'What — Hissing Sid, the evil snake,' said Rat, 'whose great-great-great-great-great-granddad started all the trouble?'

'That wasn't his fault,' said Owl. 'I say we give him a chance.'

'I agree,' said Captain Beaky. 'There are five of us. All right, Sid,' he called, 'you can come in. But one false move and we'll tie you in a knot and throw you in the river.'

'So kind,' hissed Sid and, slithering under the side of the boat, he curled himself up in the corner.

Toad moved behind Reckless Rat and, putting his thumb to his nose, he made a rude sign at Sid.

'That'll do,' said Owl, 'for, as Jesus said, we must love our enemies and pray for people who hurt us, for they are the ones who need help, because there's nothing special in just being good and loving those who love you. We must feel sorry for Sid. He doesn't know any better than to steal things.'

'What's stealing?' hissed Sid.

'There you are,' said Owl, 'he doesn't know.'

'Tell us,' said Captain Beaky, 'what's your most favourite possession?' Hissing Sid scratched his head with his tail and said, 'Haven't got one.'

'Well, if you had and someone took it, what would you do?'

'Swallow them,' hissed Sid.

'It's no use,' said Toad. 'He's just bad.'

'People who are well,' said Owl, 'don't need a doctor. Sid is not well and needs help.'

'Thank you,' hissed Sid. 'Are there any biscuits?'

'Chocolate ones,' said Captain Beaky, taking a packet from the basket.

Sid swallowed one so quickly that they could all see it going down.

'Now pay attention,' said Owl, 'because I'm going to read you an important parable that Jesus told.'

'What's a parable?' said Bat.

'It's a story within a story,' said Owl. 'A farmer got a handful of seeds and threw them into the air. The wind blew them, and some fell on stony ground, and some among weeds, and some on nice fresh soil. The ones on stony ground died, and the ones among the weeds got tangled up and died, and the ones that fell on fresh soil grew into strong wheat.'

'You didn't say it was wheat,' said Bat, 'Just seeds.'

'You are typical stony ground,' said Owl. 'Is there any fresh soil listening?'

'Yes,' said Captain Beaky. 'The story means some people benefit from learning and some don't.'

'Wouldn't it have been easier to say that,' asked Rat, 'instead of all that mumbo-jumbo?'

'Mumbo-jumbo, as you call it,' said Owl, 'makes people work things out for themselves.'

'If they have the brains to work them out,' said Toad.

'You will understand this,' said Owl. 'The seeds represent ideas of what is good and what is bad. The words of Jesus are told to everyone, but some don't listen and some don't understand or even try to. But the reason why Jesus did all those miracles was so that the people would believe that he really was the son of God, and if they believed that, then they would believe in God and goodness. They'd be kind, and they'd forgive people who had been unkind, and they'd try not to be greedy, and they'd help people who were less fortunate. And if they believed in God, then they would live for ever in heaven, and the kindest and gentlest of them would be the most popular when they got there.'

'Heaven — never heard of it,' said Hissing Sid.

'That doesn't mean that it isn't there,' said Captain Beaky.

'Well,' said Sid, 'will I go to heaven when I die?'

'No,' said Rat. 'Definitely not.'

'Then I don't want to waste my time here,' hissed Sid.

'Hold on,' said Owl. 'Since when has Reckless Rat decided who does and who does not go to heaven?'

33

'Sid's not good enough to go to heaven,' said Rat.

'I agree,' said Captain Beaky.

'That goes for me too,' said Toad.

'And me,' squeaked Bat.

'Have all of you,' asked Owl, 'been so good all your lives that there's not one bad thing you have done — not *one* thing that you can think of?'

'Well, er — maybe one,' said Rat.

'Well, perhaps one and a half,' said Captain Beaky.

'Well, little things that no one knows about,' said Toad.

'I can't remember anything,' said Bat, 'except telling a fib occasionally, and then I probably didn't.'

'What's the difference,' asked Owl, 'between one bad thing and a lot of bad things?'

'Twenty-three,' said Bat. 'I'm only guessing, of course.'

'It appears that none of us are perfect,' hissed Sid.

Captain Beaky looked rather anxious. 'You mean none of us will go to heaven if we've made a mistake?'

'We all make mistakes,' said Owl. 'Even I do. And of course God forgives mistakes.'

'Just as well,' said Rat, ''cos you made the biggest one today. You were responsible for frightening all the people away.'

'I've already admitted that,' said Owl. 'Now, if I can get back to the story, the important thing is that Jesus did lots of miracles so that people would take notice. If, on the other hand, he had managed to get all the people in the world together in the same place, he would have had to do only one big miracle to convince them who he was and, having done that, to get them to believe in what he said.'

'I've got a question,' said Toad. 'To save all this trouble of having to walk about everywhere and go through all these different things like starving and being tempted, why didn't God . . . if he was so powerful, why didn't God just appear to everyone, you know, as tall as the sky, to frighten them and tell them to be good? That's what I would have done.'

'Up till now,' said Owl, 'I thought you were following the story quite well, but I see you have missed the whole point.'

'Oh,' said Toad, wishing he hadn't spoken.

'I agree,' said Rat.

'In that case,' said Owl, 'perhaps you would like to explain what I mean.'

'No, no,' said Rat. 'You're doing a good job. You carry on.'

'The point is,' said Owl, 'that for God to show everyone on earth that he was their father in heaven, he sent his son to appear on earth as an ordinary man — except that this ordinary man was filled with the Holy Spirit. Nevertheless, he ate, slept and felt cold and pain just like you and I, and he had sandals just like Timid Toad's.'

'I thought they were a bit big,' said Rat.

'His purpose,' said Owl, ignoring the interruption, 'was to show all the people that an ordinary man could be loved by God, and that if people lived in a way that pleased God, they would find lasting happiness. Apart from which, it's clear from the story that God didn't make things easy for Jesus. He was as poor as the poorest man. He had nowhere more special to sleep than the foxes in their holes or the birds in their nests, and even the lilies of the fields wore better and brighter clothes than he did. But he wasn't unhappy because he was loved.'

'Unlike Sid here,' said Rat, 'who is not loved by anyone.'

'I wish I *was* loved,' said Sid, and for the first time ever a big tear ran down his cheek. 'I don't mean to be bad really. I just make mistakes.'

The assembled company were quite speechless.

Timid Toad was the first to speak. 'Have the rest of the chocolate biscuits,' he said.

'I'm not good enough for them,' said Sid, and burst into tears.

'Here's my hanky,' said Rat. And Sid blew his nose so long and so noisily that Rat said he could keep it. There was an awkward pause.

'What about the bit where he walked on the water?' said Timid Toad. 'I like that story.'

'That was to convince his friends that he was who he said he was,' said Owl. 'You see, they kept doubting him.'

'But they'd seen all his miracles,' said Captain Beaky, 'so how could they?'

'Oh, they didn't doubt he could do miracles,' said Owl, 'but once you've seen one you've seen them all. When he walked on the water it was also to test his followers.'

'How?' said Rat.

'You will recall,' said Owl, 'that he asked one of them, Simon, to walk on the water as well. So Simon stepped on to the water and walked towards Jesus. But halfway there he suddenly realized what he was doing, and because he doubted for a moment that he could walk on the water, he found he couldn't and sank. And Jesus reached out a hand and pulled Simon up, and told him that if he had more faith and trust in him, he wouldn't have sunk. Which means that if you believe in God, anything is possible, but if you only half-believe, only half is possible.'

'Well,' said Captain Beaky, 'if I kept doing miracles and people didn't listen to what I had to say, then I'd get pretty fed up with them.'

'But would you give up?' said Owl.

Captain Beaky thought for a moment. 'No,' he said. 'I'd do something really big to convince them and *then* I'd give up.'

'Well, that's what Jesus did,' said Owl, 'except he never gave up. The people followed Jesus everywhere, and they listened to him more than anybody else. And the government thought that if this went on, they wouldn't be able to control the people, and the priests were cross because the people weren't listening to them.'

'I expect the government were worried about the next election,' said Rat.

'They didn't have elections two thousand years ago,' said Owl. 'The stronger people made the weaker ones work for them.'

'Why didn't they go on strike?' said Bat. 'I would.'

'Because,' said Owl, 'if they didn't do what they were told, they were put to death.'

'I can see that would end a strike pretty quick,' said Rat.

'Well,' said Owl, 'while they were worrying about Jesus, he gathered more and more people around him, healing the sick and telling them how to lead a good life by caring less about earthly things and more about spiritual ones.' Owl paused and licked his lips. 'I'm very thirsty,' he said. 'Is there any lemonade?'

Captain Beaky cautiously opened the lid of the picnic basket and peered inside. 'Very little,' he said. Timid Toad quickly popped his head over the edge of the basket.

'Oh look,' said Toad, 'two bottles of lemonade, lots of biscuits, two pots of jam, six bags of crisps and a big bar of chocolate.'

'That's my emergency supply,' said Captain Beaky firmly, closing the lid. Just in time Timid Toad put his hand in, grabbed the chocolate and held it above his head to show how big it was. Before they could stop him, Hissing Sid snatched the chocolate bar in his mouth, wriggled out of the boat and disappeared into the darkness.

'After him!' shouted Rat. 'He's got our chocolate bar.'

'*My* chocolate bar,' said Beaky.

'It's very dark out there,' said Toad.

'Follow me,' said Captain Beaky. 'We'll get him.'

And with Reckless Rat, Bat and Toad close behind, he rushed out into the night. Owl, who'd got cramp in his left leg, stayed where he was and, opening a bottle of lemonade, had a long, satisfying drink. After a few minutes he heard a loud yell, then silence. Then a triumphant Captain Beaky, Toad and Bat appeared, followed by Reckless Rat.

'Got it back,' said Rat, waving the bar of chocolate in the air.

'Sid got tangled up in a bush,' said Toad, 'so I jumped on his tail and he let it go.'

Sitting down, they broke the chocolate into five pieces and shared it out.

'Where were we in the story?' said Bat, 'I forget.'

'We were,' said Owl, passing the lemonade, 'at the bit where we put less value on earthly possessions than on spiritual ones. Has it occurred to you that, apart from a chocolate biscuit, Sid probably hasn't eaten for days?'

'He could have asked,' said Rat.

'He didn't have to steal it,' said Toad.

'He doesn't know any better,' said Owl.

Captain Beaky took off his hat and held it out.

'Let's put back the bits we haven't nibbled and I'll leave them outside.'

'If I give you mine, will I go to heaven?' asked Bat.

'Oh yes,' said Rat, 'I can see it all now. "Who have we got here today?" asks God. "Batty Bat," says Jesus. "He gave up eating a piece of chocolate." "Really?" says God. "Does this mean we're letting just anybody in now?"'

'Oh, all right,' said Bat, 'he can have half,' and after taking a bite he dropped a small piece into the hat. Captain Beaky took the hat outside and gave a piercing whistle. Cupping his hands, he shouted, 'Come back, Sid. THERE'S SOME CHOCOLATE HERE FOR YOU.'

They all listened but heard no reply. Timid Toad picked up the telescope and peered into the darkness. 'Not a sign of him,' he said.

'Leave it outside,' said Owl, 'and we'll see if he comes for it.'

'Shall we leave some lemonade for him as well?' said Toad.

'No,' said Owl, taking another drink from the bottle, 'there's plenty of water in the river if he's thirsty.'

'Is that what is called being half-good?' said Captain Beaky. 'You know, chocolate but no lemonade?'

Owl handed the bottle to Captain Beaky. 'Put half a bottle of lemonade outside,' he said and, uncorking another one, he passed it round.

'You're being very generous with my lemonade,' said Captain Beaky, as he put the bottle beside Sid's share of the chocolate.

'I expect they're making a note of it up in heaven,' said Rat.

'Now,' said Owl, 'while we are having our biscuits and lemonade, I'll get on to the next part of the story.'

'It's very long,' said Batty Bat. 'I keep forgetting bits.'

'Then I'll remind you,' said Owl, 'in very simple words that even a bat can understand. God made the world and put people on it. But the people didn't appreciate the world and were cruel to each other and generally made a mess of things. Although they believed in God, they really didn't pay much attention to him, so he sent his son down to remind them. Those who heard Jesus's words and recognized the truth in them were sorry about their sins and tried to do better. But lots of others didn't believe he was who he said he was, despite all the miracles.'

'Rather like us doing good things in the Woods,' said Captain Beaky. 'Not everyone in the Woods is pleased to see us.'

'True,' said Owl, 'and what's more, doing good is a great responsibility because everyone's waiting for you to make a mistake.'

'Like banging our sticks on the biscuit tin,' said Rat.

'One mistake,' said Owl, 'and everyone remembers it.'

'Except me,' said Bat. 'I'd forgotten.'

'Now the next part of the story is very sad,' said Owl, 'because Jesus knew that lots of powerful people thought that he was becoming too important, and they wanted him out of the way. He knew he was going to be killed.'

'Well, if he knew,' said Toad, 'why didn't he run away?'

42

'Because he was very brave,' said Owl. 'And he knew that if he appeared in front of his friends after he died, then everyone who heard about it would realize that death isn't the end of everything. They would understand what he meant when he told them about life for ever — especially for those who had led a good life. Now, that doesn't mean that they had to be as good as Jesus, but they had to do their best.'

'I hope God knows I do my best,' said Rat anxiously.

'I always mention you in my prayers,' said Toad. 'I always tell God that you are doing your best, and it's not your fault you keep getting into trouble and fighting everyone.'

'Leave me out of your prayers,' said Rat. 'God's bound to get hold of the wrong end of the stick the way you explain things.'

'What is very clear to me,' said Captain Beaky, 'is that it must have been a terrible responsibility for Jesus to be the son of God.'

'It was,' said Owl. 'And he was very worried about it because he always knew what was going to happen before it did.'

'I wondered about that,' said Rat. 'How did he know?'

'He was in contact with God,' said Owl.

'Well,' said Bat, 'how did God know what would happen before it did?'

'Because,' said Owl, 'God can look down and see farther than anyone else.'

'You mean,' said Bat, 'rather like me being at the top of a tree when someone's coming down the path towards you, and you can't see them but I can, and when I tell you, you know about it before they appear?'

'For once,' said Owl, 'you're absolutely right.'

And Bat was so pleased that he leapt up and down flapping his wings, shouting 'Yippee! Got it!'

'Now,' said Owl, 'while the soldiers searched the countryside for Jesus, he and his twelve friends were staying in a house in a town called Jerusalem. One evening, as they were all sitting around a big wooden table eating bread, drinking wine and talking, Jesus said to them, "This will be our last supper together because tonight one of you will hand me over to the soldiers." There was silence at the table, then they all asked at once who would do such a thing, but Jesus wouldn't say. While the others were busy talking to each other, Jesus turned to his friend Peter and said quietly, "Before the cock has crowed twice tonight, you will say three times that you don't know me."

Peter shook his head and said that he would rather die than pretend not to know Jesus. When they had finished the bread and wine, Jesus said, "Let's go for a walk," and he took them to the gates of a lovely garden called Gethsemane, and he told them to wait while he went in to pray. Now the reason he asked them to wait outside was because he was very upset and he didn't want them to see him crying.'

Rat swallowed. 'A good person like that shouldn't have to cry,' he said. 'I wish I'd been there to help him.'

'All his best friends were there,' said Owl, 'but Jesus wanted to be alone in the garden so he could talk to God privately. And as he knelt on the soft green grass, he said to God, "Do I have to go through all this?" And God said, "Yes, I know it's hard, but it's the only way we can help everyone." And God explained that it wasn't only for the people who lived just then, but for their children as well, and their children's children, and it was up to Jesus to be a good example, even for us all these years later.' And Owl put the book down on his knees and polished his spectacles.

'I'd forgotten how upsetting it was,' said Captain Beaky in a hoarse voice and, lighting another candle, he stuck it in the top of the now empty lemonade bottle.

'Perhaps you've heard enough for tonight?' said Owl.

'No, no,' said Rat, 'go on. It's just like being there — I can imagine that lovely garden with the grass and the smell of all the nice flowers on a warm night, and poor Jesus having a cry 'cos he knew it was the last lovely garden he'd be in.'

'It was,' said Owl, 'because when he came out, one of his friends, Judas, arrived with the soldiers and pointed Jesus out to them, and they paid Judas thirty pieces of silver as a reward.'

'I'll never understand people,' said Timid Toad. 'How could he have done that?' And Toad looked very sad.

'All the disciples ran away,' said Owl, 'and Jesus was taken to prison. Outside the prison Peter tried to see if he could catch a glimpse of Jesus so he could give him a wave, and one of the people in the large crowd that had gathered there said, "Here, aren't you Jesus's friend Peter?" And Peter said, "Who, me? No, I've never heard of him," and started to run away.'

'Fibber,' said Rat.

'And then someone else asked him the same question, and again Peter said that he didn't know Jesus. The third time he denied that Jesus was his friend, Peter heard a cock crow twice, just like Jesus had said it would. Then the soldiers were ordered to bring Jesus to the Governor of the land, who was called Pontius Pilate, so that the Governor could decide what should happen next. But before Jesus arrived, the priests went to see Pontius Pilate. They wanted to get rid of Jesus because he was more popular than they were, and they asked the Governor to condemn him to death.'

'But he hadn't done anything wrong,' said Toad. 'I don't understand why they wanted to hurt him when he was so kind to everybody.'

'They were jealous,' said Rat. 'People who aren't liked are always jealous of people who are.'

'Well,' said Owl, 'Pilate could see that Jesus was a good man. As far as he could tell, the only crime Jesus was accused of was being like a king to the ordinary people.'

'What was wrong with being an ordinary people's king?' asked Rat.

'Well,' said Owl, '*king* sounds higher than *priest*, and the priests didn't like that. Pilate didn't want to hurt Jesus, but he didn't want to anger the priests either, so he gave in to them and agreed that Jesus should be put to death on a cross, like an ordinary criminal. So poor Jesus was taken outside, where a large crowd was waiting. As all the people shouted and jostled each other for a better view, the soldiers said to Jesus, "So some of these people think that you're a king, do they? Well, we'd better make you look like one!" And on his head they placed a crown of sharp thorns, and around him they wrapped a big purple robe. And then they lifted a heavy wooden cross on to his back and made him carry it through the streets. And as he walked slowly past the crowds that lined the way, they jeered at him and hit him with sticks, and they laughed each time he fell.'

Toad burst into tears. 'Fancy laughing at him,' said Toad. 'How could they?'

'He forgave them,' said Owl, 'even though they stood his cross up on top of a hill called Calvary, which overlooked the town, and then nailed his hands and feet to it. Jesus said to God, "Forgive them, Father, because they don't know what they are doing." And at noon a black cloud hid the sun and the world went dark.'

'God did that?' asked Rat in a whisper, and then he noticed that even brave Captain Beaky was having a cry. So he had one too.

'There was a thief next to Jesus on another cross,' Owl went on, 'and a thief on the other side as well, and one of them said to Jesus, "Here, you, if you're supposed to be the son of God, why don't you save yourself and me too?" But the other thief said, "Don't take any notice of him, Lord. We should be here because we really are bad people, but you shouldn't." And Jesus turned to him and said, "When I get to heaven you will be sitting there with me because you are a good man."'

Owl paused because his voice was a bit shaky.

'That was a nice thing for Jesus to say,' said Batty Bat very quietly.

'Yes,' said Owl, clearing his throat, 'it was. Jesus was always kind to people.' And he nodded at Bat in a friendly way because Bat didn't always understand things so clearly.

'And then at three o'clock,' said Owl, 'Jesus looked up to heaven and asked his father why he hadn't helped him because he was very unhappy. And he called in a loud voice, "Why have you abandoned me?" Then he died.' There was a long silence.

'Had God abandoned Jesus?' asked Rat.

'No,' said Owl, 'but Jesus was in such pain that he didn't want to live any longer. You see, he'd done everything God had asked him to do, and he just wanted to rest. And a few minutes later a soldier came and stuck a spear in his side just to make sure that he was dead, and at that moment a huge curtain in the temple ripped from end to end, and there was an earthquake that shook the land. And the people were afraid because they knew that God was angry, and that Jesus *was* his son, and that the best and kindest person in the world had been killed.'

Owl closed the Bible and put it on his knee. Taking off his spectacles, he wiped them on his nightshirt for a long time. With a sputter the flickering candle on the picnic basket went out.

'It's time we went to bed,' said Owl.

Timid Toad tugged at Owl's sleeve. 'Can I stay at your house?' he asked. 'I don't want to sleep all on my own tonight.'

'Of course,' said Owl, replacing his spectacles.

'Me too,' said Bat.

'I, er, left my house in rather a mess,' said Captain Beaky, 'so if you have any spare room . . . ?'

'Of course,' said Owl.

'Well,' said Reckless Rat, 'if you're all going to have breakfast together at Owl's, I might as well stay there too.'

So with much cracking of knees and 'Oh, my back,' 'Ouch,' 'I've got pins and needles,' the Band crawled out from under the boat.

'My best hat!' said Captain Beaky. 'Hissing Sid's taken my best hat as well as the chocolate!'

'He definitely won't go to heaven,' said Rat.

'It's lucky I've got a spare one,' said Captain Beaky. Opening the picnic basket, he produced a rather crumpled old hat, which he banged on the side of the boat to get rid of the dust. Then, picking up the firefly lantern, he tapped on the glass, and all the fireflies woke up. In the glow of their light, Captain Beaky guided his Band back to Owl's house, through a world of dancing shadows.

'I'm going straight to bed,' yawned Owl, as he led the way up the narrow wooden staircase of the big old tree house.

'Good idea,' said Captain Beaky, tapping on the firefly lantern. 'We're home now,' he said, and all the fireflies went back to sleep.

Owl opened the door of his living-room and the others followed him in.

Rat collapsed on to the sofa. 'My poor old feet,' he said.

'Mine too,' said Timid Toad and, sitting on the arm of the sofa, he gave a loud yawn.

'Please don't sit on the arm of my best sofa,' said Owl as he wound up the cuckoo clock over the fireplace. 'It makes them go out of shape.'

'Oh, sorry,' said Toad. 'I haven't got a sofa, so I wouldn't know.'

'Now, where are we all going to sleep?' inquired Captain Beaky as he put his lantern down.

Owl gave a final wind. 'Well,' he said, 'there's comfortably room for the three of us on my big feather bed, but as there are four, not including Bat who sleeps outside, one of us will have to sleep in the little attic room at the top of the tree.'

'I think that will be a bit small for me,' said Captain Beaky, stretching himself to his full height.

'Me too,' said Rat. 'My tail gets very cold if it hangs out of bed.'

'Well, I'm not sleeping up there,' said Owl. 'The ceiling's got knot holes in it, and it's very draughty, and at my age one can't be too careful.'

They all turned and looked at Timid Toad. 'I think I've got a cold coming on,' said Toad. 'Yes, definitely a cold. In fact, I think I'm going to sneeze.' Toad took a deep breath and pretended to give a loud sneeze. 'Listen to that,' said Toad. 'It's quite a bad cold by the sound of it.'

'To be fair,' said Artful Owl, 'we'll draw lots.' Reaching behind him, he gave four separate tugs. 'I have,' he announced, 'at some inconvenience, removed four feathers from my tail. One of them is much shorter than the others and whoever chooses it gets the attic.' Holding the feathers out so that only the ends of the quills could be seen, he invited them to choose one.

'It's not fair,' said Toad. 'You know which is the shortest one.'

'You can all choose before me,' said Owl.

'Oh,' said Toad and sneezed again. 'Bad cold, this,' he said, hopefully.

'I'll go first,' said Reckless Rat.

Choosing one of the feathers, he held it up. 'It's quite a big one,' he said, looking pleased.

'My turn,' said Captain Beaky. He compared his with Rat's. 'Mine's even bigger,' he exclaimed.

'Only just,' said Rat.

'That leaves me and Toad,' said Owl.

'I'll go last,' said Toad. 'I'll just sit down while you choose because this cold has made me feel a bit giddy.' Falling backwards into the armchair, he gave the loudest sneeze he could.

Owl picked out a feather that was half the size of the other two. Toad jumped to his feet. 'Oh, bad luck, Owl,' he said. 'My turn.' Toad's feather was so small he even forgot to sneeze.

'I'll get a candle,' said Owl, and disappeared into the kitchen.

'I'll be very lonely in the attic,' whispered Toad.

'Don't worry,' said Reckless Rat. 'You'll have the wind howling through those big old knots to keep you company.'

'Oh dear,' said Toad.

'Don't worry, Toad,' said Captain Beaky, 'we'll come and tuck you in.'

'Will you really?' said Toad. 'That's very kind.'

50

'Here's a candle and a hot-water bottle,' said Owl. 'It's really quite nice up there.' And so, led by Owl holding a candle, Timid Toad, Reckless Rat and Captain Beaky climbed the narrow staircase, past Owl's bedroom with the big, comfy feather bed, and up and up until it was so narrow that Owl could only just squeeze through the doorway at the top.

The room was unpainted, and the moon shone through a big knot hole almost above the little bed. On the floor by the bed was an old bucket half-full of rain-water, and next to the bed was a small table. The sound of leaves blown by the wind and the rattle of branches reminded Toad to give his biggest sneeze yet.

'If I become ill in the night, you will hear me if I call for help?' said Toad.

'Oh, don't be silly,' said Captain Beaky. 'You'll be perfectly all right.'

'And this is a very cosy bed,' said Owl, popping the hot-water bottle in it. 'I slept in it when I was small.' Pulling back the covers, he told Timid Toad to hop in.

'It's not a bad room at all,' said Rat, stepping back and banging his head on the old gnarled wooden ceiling. 'Ouch,' he said, 'that hurt.'

'You won't leave me till I go to sleep?' asked Toad anxiously.

'Of course not,' said Captain Beaky, removing his hat and putting it on a nearby shelf. As he sat down on the edge of the bed, he took the candle from Owl and put it on the table.

'Now you'll be fine,' said Owl, settling down in a chair at the end of Toad's bed. 'You just go to sleep.'

'You'd better leave some matches,' said Toad, 'in case I sneeze and blow the candle out.'

'We'll blow it out when you've gone to sleep,' said Rat.

'I'm not very tired,' said Toad, opening his eyes as wide as he could to show how awake he was.

'You soon will be,' said Rat with a big yawn, as he sat next to Owl. 'Just try counting sheep.'

'They move so quickly, they keep me awake,' said Toad. 'I prefer counting snails.'

'If none of us speaks at all,' said Captain Beaky, 'you'll be asleep in no time.'

'I expect you're right,' said Toad. 'By the way, I did enjoy the story. I've got a much better idea of the Bible now.'

'Yes, so have I,' said Owl with a yawn.

'I was wondering,' said Toad, 'when we were walking home, where exactly do you think heaven is?'

'It's up there,' said Captain Beaky, pointing to the hole in the ceiling. 'A very long way up there.'

'But how do you know?' said Timid Toad. 'It might be sideways, not up.'

'It's up,' said Rat. 'Isn't that right, Owl?'

Owl gave an enormous yawn. 'Definitely up,' said Owl. 'It must be up because Jesus went up to heaven — he didn't go sideways.'

'But how do you know he went up?' said Toad.

'It says so in the Bible,' said Captain Beaky.

'Whereabouts in the Bible?' said Toad, propping himself up on his pillows.

'You're not going to sleep yet, are you?' said Owl.

'No,' said Toad. 'I don't think I am.'

'I'll go and get the Bible,' said Owl, 'and I'll read you a little bit about what happened after he died, if you promise to go to sleep.'

'I promise,' said Toad.

Owl returned with the Bible. He had changed into his dressing-gown and was wearing his best woolly carpet slippers. Sitting on a chair at the end of the bed, he opened the book.

'And so it came to pass,' said Owl, 'that Jesus was buried in a cave and that a big rock, which took lots of people to move it, was rolled against the entrance, and two soldiers stood guard over it.'

'Why did they do that?' said Rat. 'I mean, if the rock was that big, they wouldn't need the guards.'

'Because,' said Owl, with a yawn, 'they didn't want lots of Jesus's friends to come and roll the rock away and take his body somewhere else so that they could make a big occasion of his death. That's why they put his body in the cave in the first place — it was the most ordinary place they could think of.'

'Yes,' said Rat nodding. 'Yes, a cave certainly is an ordinary place.'

Owl yawned again. 'Go on,' said Toad. 'They put him in a cave. . . .'

'Yes,' said Owl, blinking to keep his eyes open. Peering at the book, he continued. 'It was Sunday morning,' said Owl, 'just before dawn, and the guards were nearly asleep.'

'Yes,' said Toad, 'go on.'

'Asleep . . . ,' murmured Owl, and his head dropped on to his chest, and they all heard a faint snore.

'He's dropped off,' said Rat.

'Oh dear,' said Timid Toad. 'Rat, would you mind reading just a bit? I really am quite sleepy. I think I'll fall asleep myself quite soon.'

'Well, I'm not too good at reading,' admitted Rat, looking embarrassed.

'Not too good!' said Captain Beaky. 'You can hardly read at all.'

'I'm not that bad,' said Rat. 'It's just the long words that I don't know.'

'I'll read,' said Captain Beaky.

'No you won't,' said Rat, gently taking the book from Owl's lap without waking him. 'Now, if you'll just give me a moment to glance at it . . . ' Rat peered at the book, mouthing the words as he read them. 'Some of the words are a bit long,' said Rat, 'but I think I've got the general idea.'

Reckless Rat cleared his throat and began. 'The guards were nearly asleep when two angels came down from heaven — which is up — and, getting hold of the rock, they rolled it away. And of course the guards' hair stood on end, and they ran off, and naturally the word got round pretty quick. And some of Jesus's friends, including Peter and John, came to see if it was true, and with them came some people who had been looking after Jesus's mother. One of them was called Mary Mag–, er, Mary, er . . . '

'Mary Magdalene,' said Captain Beaky, leaning across to see the page.

'Don't read over my shoulder,' said Rat. 'It puts me off.'

'Now when they got there,' continued Rat, 'there was no sign of Jesus, just the piece of cloth they'd wrapped him in.'

'Was he up in heaven?' said Toad.

'Hang on,' said Rat, 'I've got to turn the page.' He turned the page and peered at it. 'Just then,' said Rat, 'Mary saw a man standing nearby. As he was a very ordinary-looking sort of man, she thought he was a gardener or something, and she said to him, "Have you taken Jesus away? He's not here." Then the man walked up to her and said, "Hello, Mary, it's me." And she suddenly recognized him, and it was Jesus.'

'Why didn't she recognize him right away?' said Toad.

'It says here she was crying a lot,' said Rat, 'and when you're crying a lot, Toad, you can't always see things too clearly.'

'Go on,' said Toad. 'I'm so glad it was him.'

55

'So was she,' said Rat. 'Well, Jesus asked her to go and tell everyone else, and soon everybody had heard about it, including the rest of his closest friends.'

'And where were they?' asked Toad.

'The Bible doesn't give the exact address,' said Rat, 'but it seems they were all sitting in a house somewhere, discussing the news and whether it was true or not, when suddenly, from nowhere, Jesus appeared in the middle of them. Well, you can imagine — they could hardly believe it, of course. But there he was, large as life, and to prove that it was him, he showed them the wounds on his hands and feet and in his side. And he let them touch him, and he was just as real as you and me.'

'I thought he wanted to go to heaven right away,' said Toad.

'He couldn't,' said Captain Beaky. 'He had to come back to show them that if they believed in him, they could live again like him after they died.'

'But it's such a pity he had to die,' said Toad, clutching his hot-water bottle.

'Well, that's the most important bit,' said Rat. 'He died so that all the people would be forgiven. That was his last request to God, to forgive everybody their sins. "I don't mind dying, God," he said, "if you can forgive everybody for all the bad things they've done." And the reason he said that,' and here Rat put his finger on the line he was reading and bent forward, 'was because, having lived down here with everyone, he knew how hard it was to lead a good life, what with all the temptations about. And as he stood there talking to them, his friends knew without a doubt that this was the Jesus they knew and loved and that he *had* come back, just as he said he would, and they shouted and cheered and put their arms around him.'

Rat removed his finger and went on reading. 'And Jesus said to them, "Listen, tell the people how surprised and glad you were to see me tonight, and tell them that you spoke to me and touched me, and then all the men and women and children who truly believe in me will be glad as well."'

'*I'm* glad,' said Toad, 'and I've never seen him. He seems so real that I can't imagine him ever going away.' And, giving a big yawn, he closed his eyes and lay back on his pillows.

'He's fallen asleep,' whispered Captain Beaky. 'We can go now.'

Reckless Rat nodded and closed the Bible. He put his finger to his lips and carefully climbed down from the bed. Captain Beaky did the same, and they both tiptoed towards the door.

'What did Jesus do then?' asked Toad.

'I thought you'd gone to sleep,' said Captain Beaky.

'Jesus disappeared,' said Rat, as he sat down on the bed again and tried to find the right page.

'If you'd bothered to use the bookmark,' said Captain Beaky, 'you'd know where you were.'

'I'm looking for my thumb print,' said Rat.

'You should always wash your hands before you read books,' said Toad drowsily.

'I won't read at all if you start complaining,' said Rat. 'Ah, here we are. Now a few days later some of Jesus's friends were fishing by the lake, and Jesus appeared again, and among his friends was Peter who, you will remember,' said Rat, looking up and wagging a finger, 'was the one who said he didn't know Jesus when Jesus was in prison.'

'I remember,' said Toad, 'and that cock kept crowing.'

'And,' continued Rat, 'Jesus said to Peter, "Do you love me?" "Of course," Peter said, he did very much. And Jesus asked him three times, and each time Peter said he did. And he was very upset that Jesus kept asking him.'

'Why did Jesus ask him three times?' asked Toad.

'I expect,' said Rat, 'to make up for the three times Peter said he'd never heard of Jesus, to sort of cancel them out. Anyway Jesus asked them all to take care of everybody for him and to tell everyone they met about all the things he had told them, and they promised they would. Then they had a little dinner together on the shore of the lake and talked about the good times they'd had together. And he seemed so real to them as they laughed and talked that they were really sorry when he said he had to go. But it wasn't the last time they saw him because Jesus appeared lots more times to them and other people until finally it was time for him to go home. So he gathered all his friends together in a field,' said Rat, 'and as they watched, he said goodbye and floated up between two angels, and the whole sky lit up and everyone heard lovely music. And one of the angels called out and said to the people, "Don't look so sad, because one day Jesus will come back again." And they watched until he was right out of sight. And that proves,' said Rat, 'that heaven is definitely up.'

Toad nodded sleepily.

'Now, after Jesus disappeared his friends had a terrible problem because there are lots of people in the world and they don't all speak the same language. As Jesus's friends were just ordinary people like fishermen and so on, they didn't know how to get over this. So to help them Jesus performed another miracle.'

Rat peered at the page. 'Well, it doesn't say so here, but he probably got God to help him with this one because it was a very hard and very important one. Anyway, a few days later the disciples were all having a chat together on a street corner when they heard a big wind blowing.'

'Just like now,' said Toad.

'Very similar,' said Rat.

'Then they saw flames of fire appear over each other's heads out of nowhere, and the next moment they could speak all the languages in the world, so there was no one who couldn't be told the story of Jesus, and that's why we all know it so well.' Rat closed the Bible and gave another yawn. A loud snore came from Captain Beaky.

'He's dropped off,' said Toad.

'So he has,' murmured Rat, blinking sleepily, 'and Owl's fast asleep,' he whispered. 'Better not wake them up. They look so peaceful.' With a creak of knee joints Rat stood up.

'Where are you going?' whispered Toad.

'To a comfy feather bed downstairs,' said Rat and tiptoed out of the room.

'Oh,' said Toad, 'I wish I could sleep.'

Batty Bat flew down through the old knot hole that was nearly above the bed and, gripping the edge of the shelf, he swung to and fro like a pendulum, his shadow moving backwards and forwards across the wall.

'So do I,' squeaked Bat, 'but I was awake, listening.'

Captain Beaky and Owl both gave loud snores.

'Well, I'm going to try and sleep now,' said Toad. 'Goodnight.' And, putting his fingers in his ears, he closed his eyes.

'No one's said their prayers yet,' squeaked Bat, as he swung himself up on the shelf, next to Captain Beaky's hat.

Timid Toad opened his eyes.

'I'd say them for everybody,' squeaked Bat, 'but not everybody likes two kinds of jam, so you'd better do it for all of us.'

Timid Toad very carefully got out of bed in his nightshirt and knelt down.
'Er,' said Toad.
'Um,' said Toad, frowning.
'Ah yes, of course,' said Toad and, gazing up at the stars that twinkled
through the big knot hole in the ceiling, he put his hands together and said:

'Dear Jesus, if you're still awake,
I would just like to say
That though it's rained a bit down here,
We've had a smashing day.
And all of us tried very hard
To do the things we should,
Although it must be difficult
To see us in the Wood.
There's nothing much we need, of course —
Except for this and that —
So goodbye from Captain Beaky,
Owl, Rat, Toad and Bat.
Oh, and P.S. — I'm Toad.'

Timid Toad climbed back into bed. He was just about to lie down when
something occurred to him and, leaning out of bed, he looked up through
the big knot hole in the ceiling. 'And by the way,' said Timid Toad, glancing
around to make sure everyone was fast asleep, 'don't be too cross with
Hissing Sid for taking Captain Beaky's hat because he's got lots of them —
and anyway it's the wrong size. Goodnight.'